The Santa in Me

Written by   Wendy Abboud

Illustrated by   Jasmine Bennett

ISBN 978-1-63814-705-3 (Paperback)
ISBN 978-1-63814-706-0 (Hardcover)
ISBN 978-1-63814-707-7 (Digital)

Covenant Books, Inc.
11661 Hwy 707
Murrells Inlet, SC 29576
www.covenantbooks.com

To my new friends and family:

This darling interactive magical experience began for me at a very young age. Like most young children, I also pondered if I would ever meet the real Santa Claus. I can remember so well wearing my Santa hat, looking in the mirror, and seeing myself as Santa Claus. From that moment on, I always knew I wanted to be just like him. I can remember the excitement I felt each Christmas Eve as my parents tucked me into bed, and I would try to keep my eyes open as I waited for the jolly ole' guy that wears red to come to my house.

I was blessed to be part of a family who cherished doing selfless acts for others just like Santa Claus. I can remember my mother gifting to children on the school bus she drove and thanking the ones who served our country. I can remember the smell of her freshly baked cookies. I can remember meeting so many Santas through all our adventures. I can vividly remember the magical Christmas experience.

Just like my mother and Santa Claus, I also wanted to be able to deliver the same happiness that they did; I wanted to be just like them. I tell my children and all my friends that the moral of the story is about the magic within all of us. I tell them that when they wear their Santa hat, they can be just like him—if only they believe! I tell them and now you, "When you wear your Santa hat and head out on your way, give a big chuckle because now you, too, can be Santa if even just for a day."

If we all could demonstrate a little kindness, wouldn't this world be a better place? I truly believe that together we will change the world!

Would you like to join me? Would you like to be Santa Claus? Go grab your Santa hat, cozy up with a blanket, and let's read this interactive magical experience together! As we learn and discover about The Santa in Me and you, I hope and pray all my new friends and family enjoy this experience and it allows you to believe in yourself and the gift of giving just like Santa does—not only today but throughout the year!

This book is dedicated to my mom, our Mimi, *the real* Santa Claus! Thank you for never giving up on me and always believing. I love you, Mom and Dad.

With my best wishes and many thanks from my heart to yours,

Wendy Abboud

When you grow up,
what do you want to
be?

When you grow up,
what do you want to
see?

I pray for peace,
love, good health, and
cheer,

Snowy nights and
flying reindeer.

Let's think of the greatest, I think larger than me.

Let's think of the moment; would you like to join me?

The same jolly ole' guy that we all await
Just once a year on the exact same date.
Why only one night? When we could help all year—

Grant wishes, bring gifts, and spread lots of cheer.
Although I've met many in plenty of malls,
I'm not really sure of the real Santa Claus.

Momma comes in my room and says,
"Mimi, my dear, clean up your toys.
Christmas is near."

I hop in my bed and snuggle teddy tight;
   We say my prayers; Momma dims my light.
   Mimi drifts off to sleep, and she starts to see
   Her vision comes to life—Santa Claus—is it me?

7

Yes, it's me! Yes, it's you! Yes, it's them and the little elf too!

It's you, Santa Claus, that makes dreams come true.

I'm flying through the sky; it's a magical night,
Bringing cheer and smiles, I'm turning darkness to light.
What we believe and what we think's real
Is sometimes magic; it's a great ordeal.

I can smell the cookies; I see decorations abound.
I'm listening so close; I'm hearing beautiful sounds.

Would you like to join me?

Take your hand and put it up to your ear.

It's a jingle, a jangle, of flying reindeer!

I'm flying so fast; it's so much fun.

Whew wee what an adventure it's just begun!

NORTH POLE

I'm flying like Santa;
its magical guys.
 If he can do it, so
can you, and so can I!

Wearing Santa's hat made the magic so real.
We all can be Santa—YES, Santa is real!

14

Would you like to join me?

Go on, take your hands and make a big belly—
Give a big chuckle; life's a bowl full of jelly!

I wake up in excitement; it's then that I knew,

Let's come together and make dreams come true!

I run and find Momma, for I need her to know

I had the best dream; listen here—let's go!

I've watched you give with an open heart.

Now it's my turn; where shall I start?

I know we can be him; let's give it a whirl!

The smiles, the moments, together we'll bless each boy and each girl!

More giving, more kindness, more cheer we'll spread

Just like jolly ole' Santa, that man that wears red.

Let's all wear a Santa hat—it is magic you'll feel.

We *all* can be Santa—*yes, Santa is real!*

We've all had a dream and thought it was great.

Let's pretend for a day; let's imitate!

We don't have reindeer, but our feet will do.

Who needs something special? Special, just from you.

He lives inside all of us if we follow his lead.

Go on, pass it on, buy a book, let them read!

Think large, think wide, think who's in need—
A sweater, a scarf, a toy, or good deed.

Cookies or crafts, a sweet message will do.

It's the thought that counts, it's special—it's from you!

Out the door I go with a Santa hat on my head,

Off to my neighbors with fresh ginger bread.

I signed "Love, Santa," dropped my gift, and ran fast

For everyone should know imitating Santa is such a blast!

23

Track your steps—jingle, jangle away!

Congratulations! You, too, can be Santa someday!

We'll illuminate the world with all of our blessings.

We'll take turns being Santa and keep everyone guessing.

Shhhhh, don't tell; that's all the fun. Best part is, it's for everyone.

When you deliver your gift, there'll be a twinkle in your eye.

Be proud of yourself and hold your head high!

My new friends and family you must always believe

When you give, it's joy that you will receive!

Be a blessing to all and always stay kind.
Now kick back, relax, and just unwind.
Go hang your hat and sleep peacefully my dear;
Santa is in you, and Christmas is near!

Good night to my family,
Good night all my friends.

Thank you,

Santa Claus,

For always giving; and that's the end!

Certificate of

EXCELLENCE

For being the best Santa Claus

Awarded to

Month _____ Day _____ Year _____

Signed by _ *Santa Claus* _____

BELIEVE

About the Illustrator

Jasmine Bennett is a loving wife to her husband and devoted mother to their two young daughters. Jasmine spends her days ensuring her girls' lives are full of magic and wonder. When Jasmine was growing up, she loved to read and get lost in beautiful stories. When Wendy presented this wonderful story to Jasmine, she knew she wanted to be a part of bringing the magic of kindness and hope alive for you and your families. Her prayer is that you will experience a heart full of joy after reading this delightful and heartfelt story. Thank you so much to my husband, girls, parents, and the rest of my beautiful family and friends for your support.

About the Author

Wendy Abboud is a mother of two, proud wife, daughter, sister, and friend. She is a woman of faith who knows failure but chooses to believe. Wendy loves hard, thinks deep, and shows compassion to all that she meets. By creating miracles, she has been able to take a step back and see through the eyes of the innocent child.

Through personal struggles, Wendy has been impacted in a way where she truly only wants to spread kindness and give back to the world. Wendy strives to encourage all those she encounters by uplifting their spirits. She's all about the good vibes!

Wendy was raised in a small town but had big city dreams. She prays for a world in which her children will be kind, giving, compassionate, and loved. She was always known as the wild one with crazy ideas. In her big dream, she hopes and prays that we can agree to disagree, inspire through the confusion, and be the change that we want to see.

When Wendy became a mom, she began to realize that her influence as a mother was powerful and she had little eyes watching her every move. Wendy has now set forth on her dream and is pretty certain that if we start out with a giving heart we will collectively get somewhere new, bright, and better than before!

Wendy chooses to leave a little sparkle wherever she goes!

Acknowledgments

A special thank-you to my sister Amanda for all her love, help, editing expertise, and guidance. God made us sisters, and our hearts made us friends. Our journey has led us in many directions, and I look forward to becoming more than sisters, more than best friends—coauthors!

All my love and gratitude to my husband Mike for seeing me through my dreams and supporting me the entire way. Thank you, my love!

ChaCha and T, thank you for connecting us (author and illustrator) and providing your guidance, prayers, and influence in such a challenging world.

CPSIA information can be obtained
at www.ICGtesting.com
Printed in the USA
BVRC101021241021
619719BV00008B/491

9 781638 147060